The Tasty Tale of Chewandswallow

by Rick Barba
illustrated by Pete Oswald, Justin Thompson, and Andy Bialk

Simon Spotlight
New York London Toronto Sydney

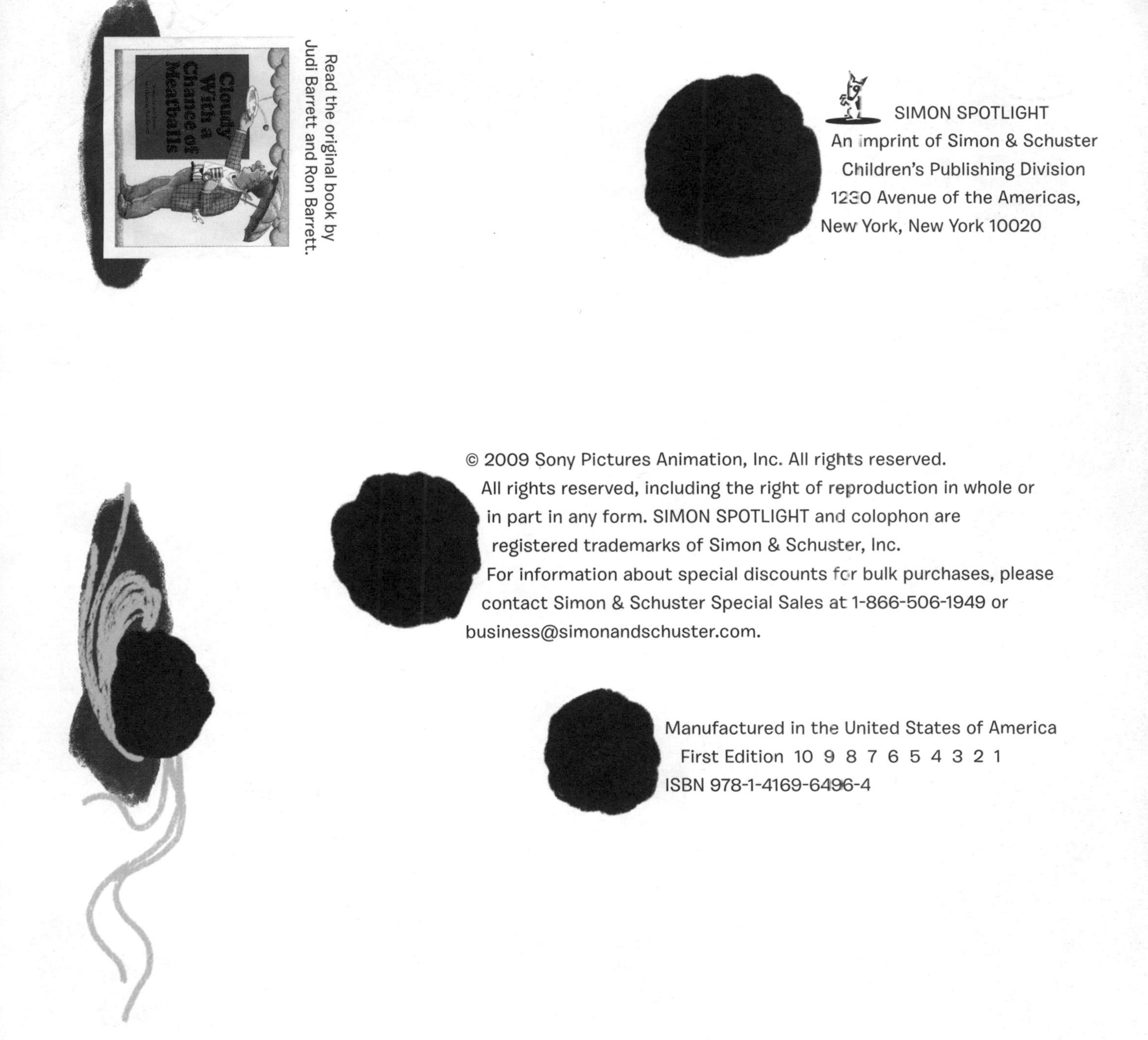

Read the original book by
Judi Barrett and Ron Barrett.

SIMON SPOTLIGHT
An imprint of Simon & Schuster
Children's Publishing Division
1230 Avenue of the Americas,
New York, New York 10020

For information about special discounts for bulk purchases, please
contact Simon & Schuster Special Sales at 1-866-506-1949 or
business@simonandschuster.com.

Manufactured in the United States of America
First Edition 10 9 8 7 6 5 4 3 2 1
ISBN 978-1-4169-6496-4

Flint Lockwood had a new invention.

"My food machine will save our town of Swallow Falls," he told Steve, his pet monkey. "This device will change water into food!"

Flint turned a few knobs on his machine before pouring water into the top. Then he typed a request into his computer. Suddenly, the bottom of the machine started bulging. Flint held his breath. Maybe this invention would be a success!

Seconds later, a huge spark exploded from the machine, and the lab fell dark and silent—once again.

"Hmm, not enough power," Flint said, still hopeful. He had been creating things ever since he was a young boy, and he never gave up on his inventions—even though a few of them didn't quite work out as planned. Flint's dad kept trying to steer him away from inventing. He wanted Flint to work with him in his tackle shop.

As a child Flint came up with Spray-On Shoes, so no one would have to worry about untied shoelaces—but he didn't come up with a way to get the shoes off.

Then there was his Flying Car, which kept crashing into things; his special Hair Un-balder tonic, which made a *little* too much hair; and his amazing Ratbirds, which kept carrying kids away.

Swallow Falls used to be famous for its Baby Brent sardines. But when people realized that sardines were disgusting, the canneries closed up.

The mayor came up with a plan to make Swallow Falls great once more—with a new theme park! The park would feature sardine rides, sardine exhibits, and the world's largest sardine, Shamo.

"Welcome to SardineLand, the greatest tourist attraction ever built," the mayor announced on opening day. "Baby" Brent, the local celebrity who appeared on the sardine cans as a baby, cut the ribbon.

A young reporter named Sam Sparks and her cameraman, Manny, came to Swallow Falls to cover the park's grand opening for WNN, the Weather News Network.

"Hello, Sam Sparks, I'm America!" she reported nervously. "I mean, uh, well . . . let's just . . . go to the mayor."

"Thank you, and welcome to Swallow Falls, home of SardineLand!" the mayor said, beaming proudly.

While everyone was at the grand opening, Flint was at the power station with his FLDSMDFR, the Flint Lockwood Diatonic SuperMutating Dynamic Food Replicator.

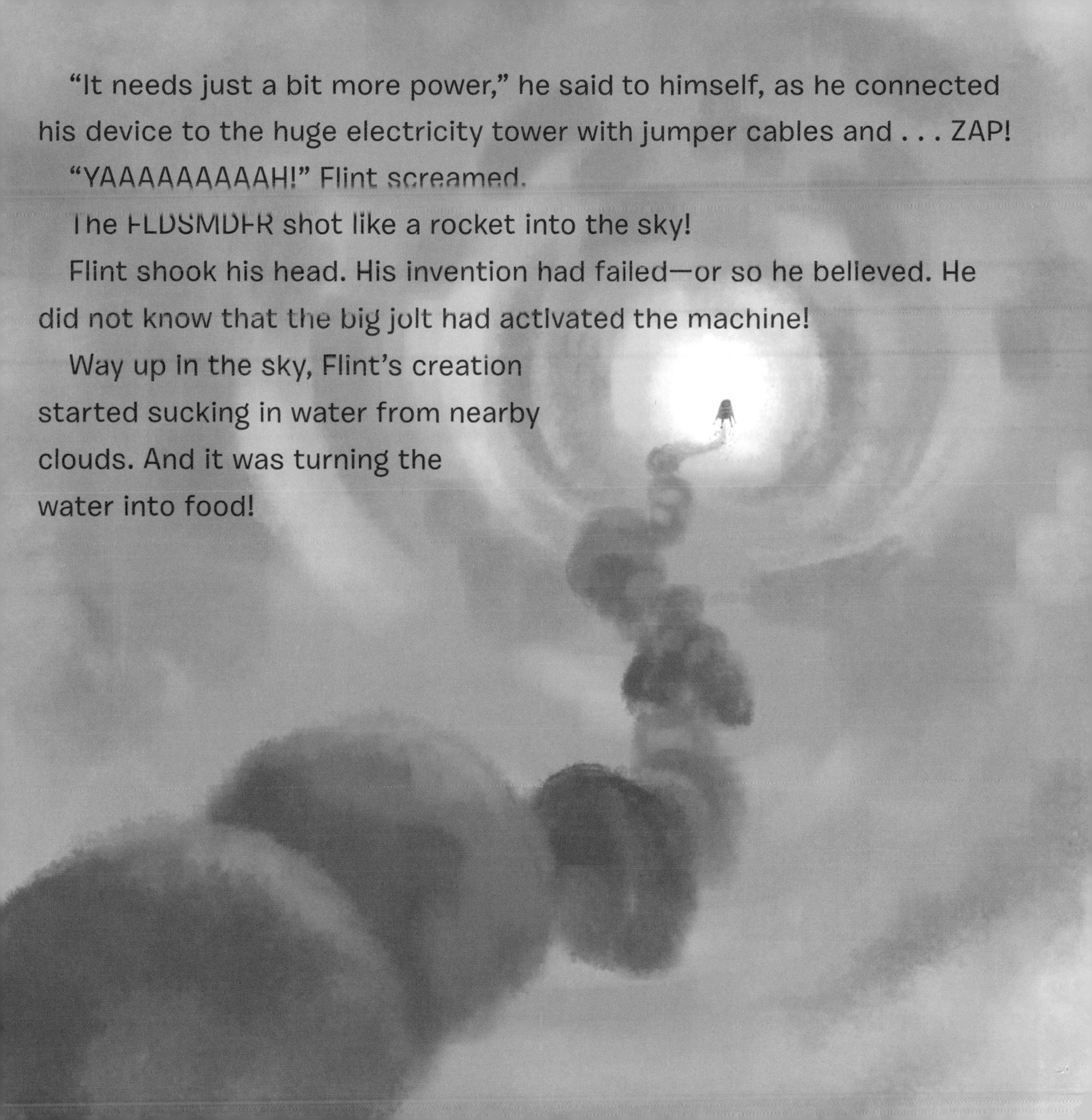

"It needs just a bit more power," he said to himself, as he connected his device to the huge electricity tower with jumper cables and . . . ZAP!

"YAAAAAAAAAH!" Flint screamed.

The FLDSMDFR shot like a rocket into the sky!

Flint shook his head. His invention had failed—or so he believed. He did not know that the big jolt had activated the machine!

Way up in the sky, Flint's creation started sucking in water from nearby clouds. And it was turning the water into food!

Suddenly, cheeseburgers began falling from the sky!

Flint couldn't believe it. "My machine works!" he shouted excitedly as he caught a cheeseburger and took a bite. "It really works!"

Sam was impressed. "These are delicious!" she reported.

Everyone in Swallow Falls rushed to grab the cheeseburgers.

Flint couldn't wait to show everyone what the FLDSMDFR could do. He started typing in food orders on his computer.

"Breakfast, coming right up," he said. "Or should I say, coming right down."

Moments later, bacon and eggs began falling from the sky!

Sam reported on WNN, "Looks like a breakfast system is on its way to Swallow Falls. My forecast: sunny-side up."

The mayor was pleased with Flint's invention. It gave him a new idea: Swallow Falls could be a "foodtopia" that tourists would flock to all year round!

"Make it rain three meals a day, every day!" the mayor told Flint.

"But I'm not sure the machine can take it," Flint replied.

"Come on, Flint," the mayor insisted. "Our falling food will bring in cruise ships packed with visitors. Everyone will love your invention!"

Flint wasn't sure, but he finally agreed. The mayor was so happy that he even changed the town's name to Chewandswallow.

Amazing goodies fell from the sky every day. Tourists gobbled pizza and hot dogs and cheese balls and jelly beans and waffles.

Police Officer Earl asked Flint to make a special treat for his son Cal's birthday. Soon the town was covered in a blanket of soft ice cream!

Flint also made a special treat for his new friend, Sam—a Jell-O castle.

"Oh, Jell-O's my favorite!" Sam exclaimed.

Flint squished himself into the jiggly castle and reached out to Sam. "Join me," he said, before pulling her in.

Sloorp! Inside, Sam and Flint jumped around on the bouncy floor.

The next day, the mayor hosted another grand opening event, this time for the grand re-opening of the town as Chewandswallow, the Food Weather Capital of the World.

Cruise ships lined the dock, and tourists filled the town square. But Flint noticed the dark clouds that were gathering in the sky. Seconds later, a three-foot-long hot dog crashed down in front of him.

"These are big hot dogs," Flint cried as more giant food began to fall from the sky.

Just then the wind picked up—a salt-and-pepper wind. Flint was hit by a giant leaf. "Oregano," he said as he sniffed the leaf. Then he looked up in time to see a huge spaghetti twister heading their way!

"MAMA MIA!" Flint yelled as giant meatballs began to smash down all around him! Everyone started to run.

Flint sprinted to his lab to shut down the FLDSMDFR, but the greedy mayor blocked his path.

"A spaghetti twister is tearing up the town!" Flint argued. "I have to turn off the machine with my shutdown recipe."

"No way, Flint," said the mayor. "I won't let you chicken out."

Flint tried to push past, but the mayor whacked him with a huge loaf of garlic bread. Then they swung oversized foods at each other—big celery sticks, enormous stalks of asparagus, and jumbo prawns.

"Food fight! Food fight!" Steve screeched.

Then the mayor used a giant beet to smash the satellite dish!

Up in space, the FLDSMDFR was going haywire. Because it was overloaded with food orders, it was now a gigantic, mile-wide food asteroid, spitting out tons of huge food items. A food storm was about to be unleashed on the entire planet!

Sam was nervous as she watched her weather radar screen. Then she reported, “Folks, this storm will wipe out everything in its path—New York, Paris, Beijing!”

"I've got to turn off the FLDSMDFR!" Flint declared. But how could he get up there?

Flint remembered his Flying Car. He quickly fixed it, then soared into the sky along with Sam, Steve, Manny, and Brent.

Suddenly, flying pizza slices attacked the car. "Hang on!" Flint shouted.

Dodging the pizza slices, he banked the car into the giant hole where the food asteroid was sucking in clouds.

Inside the food machine, Flint leaped out. Giant roast chickens stood in his path, but with Brent's help Flint managed to get past the hostile squad. Then he jumped into a spiky pit that led into the heart of the machine—and was greeted with big ears of corn shooting right at him!

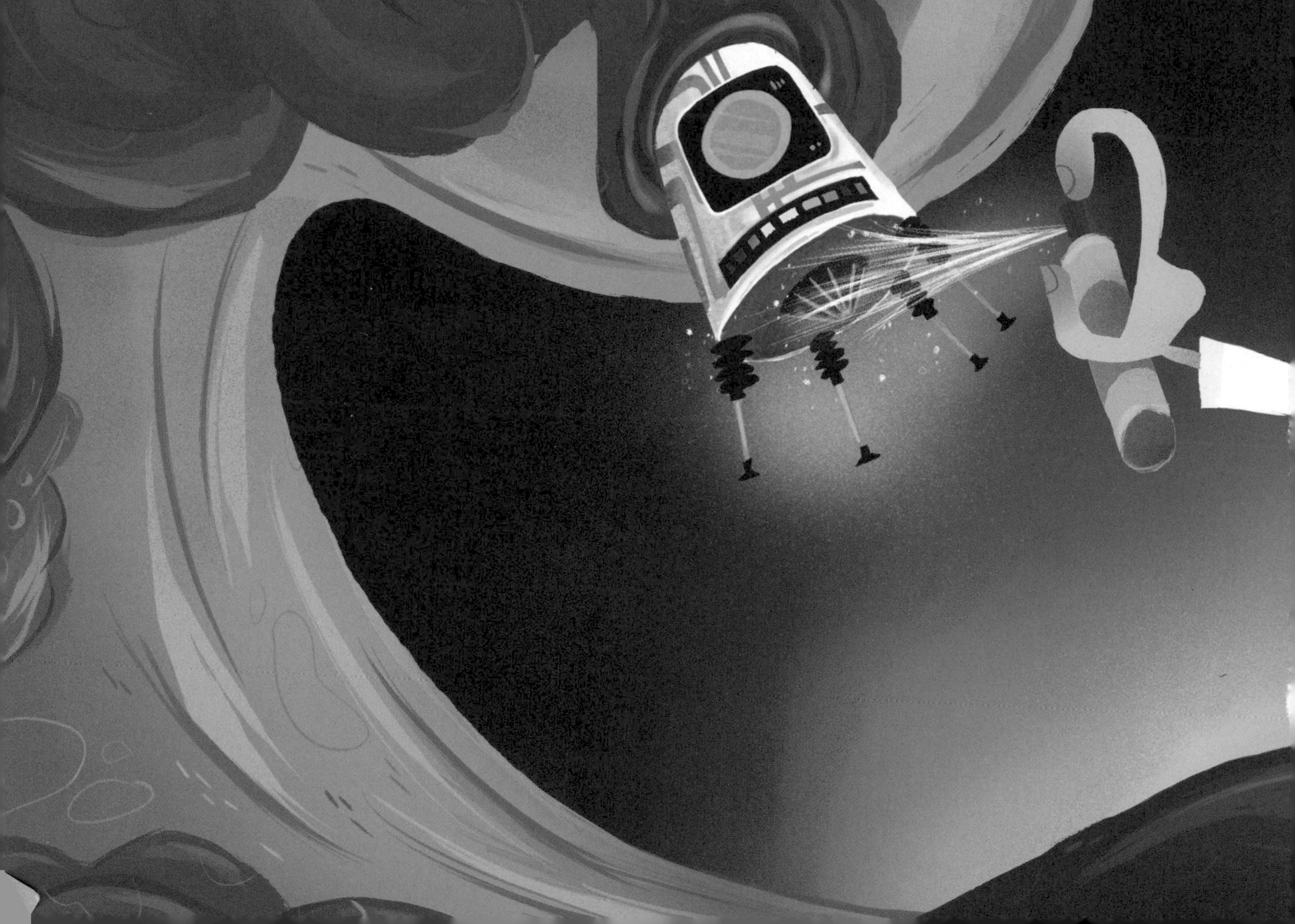

However, soon after, a flock of Ratbirds lowered Flint safely to the ground.

Sam rushed up to him. “You did it!” she said, giving Flint a big hug.

Flint had saved the world!

"Sorry, old friend," Flint said as he dove c
the way. "I've got to shut you down!"

Flint had a brainstorm. Remembering his S
Shoes that never came off, he pulled out the
spray and sealed shut the spout of the FLD

With no way to spit out its food, the mac
swelled up. It grew bigger and bigger. Fina
bulging food machine exploded!

Manny, Brent, Sam, and Steve wer
to escape to safety in the Flying Ca
it seemed like Flint had been lost
explosion.

g